Foul Play
published in 2009 by
Hardie Grant Egmont
85 High Street
Prahran, Victoria 3181, Australia
www.hardiegrantegmont.com.au

Hardie Grant Egmont uses
Greenhouse Friendly™
ENVI Carbon Neutral Paper

ENVI Carbon Neutral Paper is an Australian Government
certified Greenhouse Friendly™ Product.

The text for this book has been printed on ENVI Carbon Neutral Paper.

A CiP record for this title is available from the National Library of Australia

Text copyright © 2009 H.I. Larry
Illustration and design copyright © 2009 Hardie Grant Egmont

Cover design by Cal Bennett
Illustrations by Cal Bennett
Typeset by Ektavo
Printed in Australia by McPherson's Printing Group

3 5 7 9 10 8 6 4

TOP SECRET CODE:
CONTROL-A-BALL

TM

[24 HOURS TO SAVE THE WORLD ... AND GET TO SPORTS TRAINING]

FOUL PLAY

BY *H. I. LARRY*

ILLUSTRATIONS BY *CAL BENNETT*

hardie grant EGMONT

CHAPTER ...ONE

Zac Power's class was playing a game of soccer in PE. Zac was really good at soccer but he had to pretend he was hopeless.

One of his classmates had just kicked the ball right at him.

'Come on, Zac,' yelled Mr Kane, his PE teacher. 'Go for the ball!'

Zac jumped up to hit the ball with his

head. But he made sure he missed. Then he pretended to trip over, and crashed head-first into one of his classmates.

OOF!

The boy he'd crashed into looked annoyed, and some of the other players laughed. Zac said sorry, but he knew he hadn't hurt his classmate.

'I thought you'd been practising, Zac,' said Mr Kane, jogging over.

'I have been, sir,' said Zac.

If only I could show him what a fantastic player I really am, he thought.

Zac Power actually loved soccer. In fact, he loved most sports. He was a spy for the Government Investigation Bureau (GIB), so he had sharpened his strength and fitness on lots of dangerous missions. A GIB spy had to be ready for anything.

But no-one was allowed to know that Zac was a spy, so he had to pretend to be bad at sport.

Zac sighed as the game started again. He wished the class would hurry up and end.

Everyone at school had been crazy about soccer for the past few weeks. The National Soccer League grand final between the Superstars and the Sharks was that weekend. Zac wanted the Superstars to win. They were his favourite team.

The ball was kicked to Zac again. He

kicked it badly on purpose.

SMACK!

The ball shot off his boot like a rocket, but it didn't go anywhere near the goal. It flew out of bounds and landed in some thick bushes. Mr Kane sighed and shook his head.

'Sorry,' said Zac, his cheeks burning.

'I'm glad I signed you up for the special training session after the big game tomorrow,' said Mr Kane. 'Remember to meet me at the stadium at 3 o'clock. You'll learn a lot from training with the Superstars players.'

Zac groaned. He would have to pretend to be a terrible player again. This time would be worse though, because he'd be in front of his favourite team!

Mr Kane blew his whistle. 'That's enough for today, everyone,' he called. 'Back to the classroom! Off you go!'

Finally, thought Zac. He headed towards the school building.

'Just a minute, Zac,' called Mr Kane.

Zac stopped and turned back to his teacher.

'Please find that ball you kicked into the bushes,' said Mr Kane. 'Hurry up, the bell's about to go.'

'All right,' sighed Zac. His class and Mr Kane walked back inside. Zac was alone on the sports field.

What a horrible day, he thought. *Why can't I be called away on a cool secret mission right now?*

Zac walked over to the bushes. He couldn't see the ball anywhere. Suddenly, a strong wind whipped across the grass and around him. It sounded like thunder in his ears.

Zac looked up and saw a gigantic helicopter in the sky. It was hovering above him. Its blades were a blur, spinning like a giant fan. The helicopter was brightly painted and covered in neon lights, music speakers and fireworks launchers.

Zac grinned. Maybe his day was about to get better after all.

The helicopter landed on the grass near Zac. The door slid open and Zac's older brother Leon leant out.

'Hey, Zac,' Leon shouted above the noise. 'GIB sent me to pick you up. They need you for a mission.'

Leon was a GIB spy too, but he hardly ever went on missions. He worked in the Tech Support and Gadget Design Division. Leon was a bit of a nerd and he made awesome gadgets.

'Excellent!' said Zac. Maybe he would get out of the training session the next day after all!

Zac ducked his head under the spinning blades and ran towards Leon.

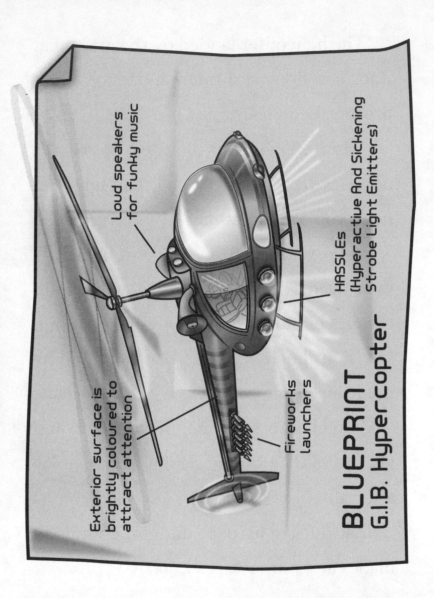

BLUEPRINT
G.I.B. Hypercopter

Loud speakers for funky music

Exterior surface is brightly coloured to attract attention

Fireworks launchers

HASSLEs
(Hyperactive And Sickening Strobe Light Emitters)

'Hey,' said Zac, climbing on board. 'What's with the fireworks and lights on this thing?'

'It's a Hypercopter,' answered Leon. 'You're going to make an entrance that no-one will forget on this mission.'

'Sounds like fun,' said Zac.

He couldn't wait to find out what sort of mission needed a fireworks-launching chopper!

CHAPTER... ...TWO

Leon took the Hypercopter's controls, and the chopper rose into the air again.

WHIRRRR

The blades whipped loudly above Zac's head. He looked out the window, watching his school oval get smaller and smaller as they took off.

'Grab your SpyPad,' Leon said, once

they were flying.

Zac pulled it out of his back pocket. He carried his GIB SpyPad at all times. It was like a phone and computer rolled into one. Zac had loads of cool games on his.

Leon handed him a small silver mission disk with the GIB logo on it. Zac slid it into his SpyPad.

CLASSIFIED – FOR THE EYES OF AGENT ROCK STAR ONLY

MISSION INITIATED: 3.00PM
CURRENT TIME: 3.17PM

The National Soccer League grand final is on tomorrow between the Superstars and the Sharks. There is a huge cash prize for the winning team and they'll also appear on TV to encourage kids to play sport.

But GIB suspects that the Sharks will cheat their way to the prize.

Your mission is to go undercover as a Superstars player and investigate. Stop the Sharks from cheating before the grand final ends at 3pm tomorrow.

MISSION TIME REMAINING:
23 HOURS 43 MINUTES
END

FOUL PLAY
>>> ON

'Is this for real?' Zac asked Leon. His stomach started doing crazy flips. 'I'm actually going to play on a National League team?'

'Definitely,' smiled Leon. 'Playing for the Superstars is the best way to get close to the Sharks without anyone suspecting.'

'Awesome!' said Zac. He felt so excited, even though he knew it was a serious mission. 'So where are we going?'

'The media are holding a big event at Bladesville Stadium this afternoon,' said Leon. 'Everyone playing in the big game will be photographed and interviewed. That includes you. And afterwards, you'll have to do a training session in the stadium.'

Zac felt like he was dreaming. *I can't believe I'll get to play alongside real soccer stars!* he thought.

Then Leon pointed to a yellow envelope. 'You'd better open that,' he said. 'It's some evidence photos from the Sharks' games this year. Notice anything strange?'

Zac picked up the envelope and shook the photos out. The pictures showed the Sharks jumping impossibly high, and other players running so fast they were just a blur.

The photos were taken from too far away for Zac to see the players' faces, but even from a distance there was something strangely familiar about their goalkeeper.

'I'm sure I know their goalie,' said Zac.

He looked closely at one of the photos. 'And there's something weird about their boots and the soccer ball.'

'Exactly,' said Leon. 'No wonder GIB is suspicious.' He pulled a lever and the Hypercopter stopped moving and hovered in the air.

'The Superstars' club building is right below us,' said Leon, 'but before we pick up the other players you should get dressed.' He threw a sports bag over to Zac.

Zac pulled a soccer shirt out of it. It was blue with a yellow star on the front.

It's my own Superstars outfit! he thought.

'I've improved the uniform for you,' continued Leon. 'It comes with a Wi-Fi

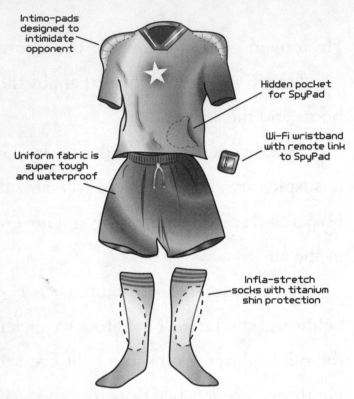

Intimo-pads
designed to
intimidate
opponent

Hidden pocket
for SpyPad

Wi-Fi wristband
with remote link
to SpyPad

Uniform fabric is
super tough
and waterproof

Infla-stretch
socks with titanium
shin protection

G.I.B. SOCCER GEAR
Professional Sports Disguise

wristband that links to your SpyPad and

watch, and Infla-stretch socks made from

a special weave of cotton and titanium.

They're lighter than conventional shin

guards, but the titanium will protect you from forces travelling at up to 300 kilometres per hour.'

'Awesome,' said Zac. Leon liked to go on about his inventions, but the uniform did sound good.

Zac put on his Superstars uniform. He looked at his reflection in a window. The yellow star on the front of his shirt flashed, catching the light.

Zac grinned. He looked exactly like a Superstars player. This was going to be his coolest mission yet!

CHAPTER... ...THREE

Then Zac remembered something. 'Leon, won't I need a disguise? All my school friends will be watching the match.'

'Yep,' said Leon. 'That's what this is for.' He pulled a jar from his bag. 'I call this Face In A Jar. It's a silicone-based compound that you use to alter your appearance. When it dries, it's the exact texture of skin.

I'll use it to make you a new nose.'

He started to spread the silicone onto Zac's face.

'Yuck!' said Zac, squirming away. It felt disgusting, like Leon had smeared mud on his skin.

'Stop wriggling,' said Leon. 'It will dry in a second and stick to your face.'

Zac groaned. *The things I do for GIB,* he thought.

When Leon was done, he held up a mirror to Zac's face. Zac looked at Leon's handiwork. Leon had given him a massive nose. It was too pale though — nowhere near Zac's skin colour.

'Leon,' Zac began. Then he stopped. The nose was changing colour as he watched! In a few seconds it matched Zac's skin colour perfectly. He looked like a completely different person.

'That's amazing, Leon,' said Zac, admiring his disguise.

'Yes, the silicone has a chameleon enzyme that matches the colour surrounding it,' said Leon. 'I think I should change your hairstyle too, just to be safe.'

'Don't even think about it,' warned Zac. No-one touched his hair!

'Fine,' said Leon, rolling his eyes. 'You do it.'

Leon handed Zac a tube of hair gel. Zac moulded his hair into tall spikes, almost like a mohawk. *Cool*, he thought, satisfied.

Then Zac glanced out the window. He could see a group of Superstars players gathered on the ground below.

Leon lowered the Hypercopter to the ground. Zac slid open the door and the Superstars climbed inside.

'Hi,' said one player. Zac recognised him — it was Sid Spikes, the Superstars' best defender. 'Are you the new player?' he asked Zac.

'Yeah,' said Zac. 'My name is ... Zav Powski. I'm from the reserves.'

'Good to have you on the team. It's funny though, I thought I knew all the reserves players,' said Sid.

'Hi, everyone,' interrupted Leon, 'I've

been asked to take you to the media event at Bladesville Stadium.'

Zac looked at his watch as the Hypercopter took off again, heading for Bladesville Stadium. He wondered if he would have time to investigate before the media event.

It took a while to get to the stadium. Zac and the Superstars players chatted and joked around.

By the time the Hypercopter was hovering over the stadium, Zac felt like one of the team. He looked out the window and saw a crowd of people gathered on the soccer field below. Some of them were Sharks players. The others were holding cameras and microphones.

'OK, everyone,' said Leon, 'it's time to enter Hyper Mode!'

Leon flipped a big switch and fireworks began shooting off the Hypercopter in all directions. Lights flashed and dance music screamed out of the Hypercopter's speakers. Zac usually hated dance music, but he couldn't help grinning with excitement.

As they flew down, Zac saw the TV cameras turn away from the Sharks to film the Superstars arriving. The photographers were going crazy, taking photo after photo of the Hypercopter.

The Hypercopter landed on the grass, sending a gust of wind over the crowd. The engine stopped and the Hypercopter fell suddenly silent and still. The crowd was frozen to the spot.

Then Leon's voice boomed out of the speakers. 'Ladies and gentlemen, I give you the SUPERSTARS!'

BOOM BOOM BOOM!

The door flew open. Zac and the other players ran onto the field, waving and cheering as the music blared again. Cameras flashed and reporters rushed forward to talk to the team.

'How does it feel to join the Superstars?' a reporter asked Zac.

'Great,' answered Zac, as reporters and players swarmed around him. 'They're the most talented team in the league.'

'Do you think the Superstars can win?' the reporter asked.

'The Sharks don't have a chance,' answered Zac. *Not if I have anything to do with it!* he thought.

After the interviews, the players lined up to have their team photo taken. The Superstars went first. Zac's face got tired from smiling for so long. The photographers' flashes started to hurt his eyes. Finally, after the photographers had asked for 'Just one more!' about ten times, the Superstars were allowed to go. The Sharks took their place in front of the photographers.

It was the first time Zac could take a good look at the Sharks. He scanned their faces. At that moment the Sharks' goalkeeper turned towards him.

Zac gasped. It was Caz Rewop, Zac's arch-enemy! She had a boy's wig on but he'd know that face anywhere. Caz worked for the evil spy agency, BIG. Zac scanned the rest of the players, but he didn't recognise anyone else.

Caz caught Zac staring at her and frowned.

Zac looked away, not wanting to draw attention to himself. As soon as the photographers were done, Caz walked through the crowd of people towards him. Zac knew he was well disguised, so he wasn't worried.

'So you're the new guy,' she sneered.

'Yep. I'm Zav,' said Zac, as politely as he could manage.

Caz smiled as the cameras kept flashing, but her eyes were cold. 'Good luck,' she said. Then she added quietly, 'Because you're going to need it.'

CHAPTER... ...FOUR

Zac clenched his fists as Caz walked back to her team. He wanted to race after her, but he couldn't blow his cover.

Now that he knew Caz was playing for the Sharks, he was sure there was something dodgy going on. But why did BIG want to win the grand final so badly? It didn't make any sense. Zac had to get to the bottom of it.

Once the reporters and TV crews had left, it was time for both teams to start their training sessions. Zac saw Leon heading back to the Hypercopter, and he gave him a quick wave goodbye.

Leon climbed into the chopper and a moment later it roared up into the sky.

Zac followed his team mates across the field. They headed towards a wide walkway that led under the grandstand.

Thousands of seats rose high above them. Zac thought of the huge crowd that would be watching them play tomorrow.

His whole body tingled.

Zac strolled down the walkway. There was a long corridor lined with giant posters of the greatest soccer players of all time. A little way along the corridor to the right was a door with 'Superstars' written on it. To his left he could see another door labelled 'Sharks'. He went right, following the rest of the Superstars to their change room.

There were tall lockers along the change room wall. Zac threw his bag into an empty one. He checked to see that no-one was looking at him. Everyone was busy putting on shin guards and soccer boots. Zac held down a button at the top of each of his infla-stretch socks. The socks inflated to look exactly like the shin guards the others were wearing.

Zac turned on his Wi-Fi wristband and tucked his SpyPad into the secret pocket in his shirt.

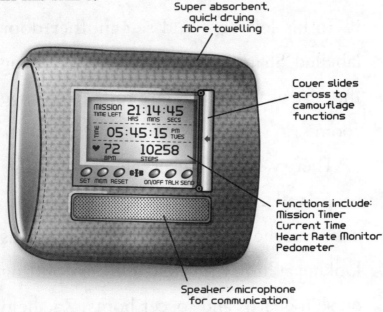

Super absorbent, quick drying fibre towelling

Cover slides across to camouflage functions

Functions include:
Mission Timer
Current Time
Heart Rate Monitor
Pedometer

Speaker / microphone for communication

G.I.B. WI-FI WRISTBAND
Sweat-absorbing Communication Device

'So, Zav,' said Sid Spikes, 'I hope you're ready to play hard. The Sharks have been winning by huge margins. Their goalkeeper hasn't let a single ball past him since he joined the team.'

Their goalkeeper's not even a 'him'! thought Zac. *But I can't tell Sid that. It might compromise my mission.*

'Don't worry,' said Zac. 'I know we can do it.'

PEEEEEEEP!

The team's coach was standing in the doorway, blowing a whistle. Zac had seen him on the sidelines of the Superstars' games.

Zac sprang up, ready for training.

He couldn't wait to test his skills.

'Hi, Coach. I'm Zav Powski,' Zac said.

Coach looked down at him. 'Hi, Zav. You come very highly recommended from the coach of the reserves,' he said. 'It's funny I've never heard of you. It's like you came out of nowhere!'

'I haven't, er, been there long,' said Zac, hoping the coach wouldn't ask too many questions.

'Well, it's good to have you on the team,' said Coach. 'Let's see what you've got!'

Zac threw his sports bag over his shoulder and ran up the walkway to the playing field. The Superstars were training on one half of the field, the Sharks on the other. Zac looked over and saw Caz defending every ball being kicked at her. He had to admit she was a good goalie.

As he watched, Zac thought he saw a ball change direction very slightly as it flew through the air towards the net. That was impossible though – maybe it was just a trick of the stadium's bright lights?

The Superstars began dribbling the ball around coloured cones. Zac weaved the ball around the cones like a pro. Then Coach got them to juggle the ball with their feet, bouncing it off their knees and heels. Zac popped his ball up in the air and kicked it into the back of the goal net. It felt so cool to show off what he could do.

The training session went quickly. The sky was completely black by the time they'd finished. Zac hadn't even noticed it getting dark — the lights at the stadium made it as bright as day.

'Great training, Zav,' Coach said to Zac as the team packed up the balls.

'Thanks,' said Zac, looking across the field at the Sharks. They were still training. *This is my chance to check their change room for anything suspicious*, he thought. He turned back to the coach. 'I guess I'll see you tomorrow for the big game.'

'What are you talking about?' said Coach. 'I'll see you on the team bus in ten minutes. We have to get to our hotel for an early night's sleep.'

Zac groaned inwardly. He should have known that the coach of a National League team wouldn't leave his players alone the night before the grand final. Still, maybe ten minutes would be enough time to check out the Sharks' change room.

Zac checked the time on his Wi-Fi wristband's screen.

He ran towards the ramp to the change rooms, keeping an eye on the Sharks at the other end of the field. They were incredible. Some were running and jumping like super heroes. Others were kicking soccer balls at their goals. The balls moved like they were being steered through the air.

There's something seriously weird going on here, Zac thought. *I've never seen players who can run and kick like that!*

Zac turned away and jogged down the ramp. Checking to see that no-one was around, he turned left and ran to the Sharks' change room. He peeked inside. It was empty.

Zac saw a pair of spare soccer boots lying on the floor. He picked one up. It had

'Boost Boot' written on the side of it. All along the bottom of the boot was wiring like a computer.

The boots were anything but ordinary soccer boots. *No wonder the Sharks can run so fast and jump so high,* thought Zac. *Their boots are computer-powered!*

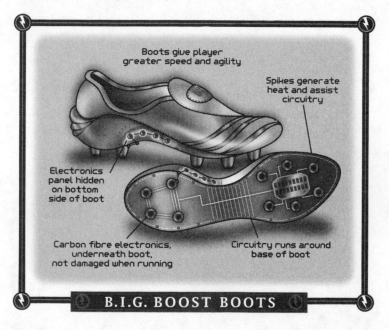

Boots give player greater speed and agility

Spikes generate heat and assist circuitry

Electronics panel hidden on bottom side of boot

Carbon fibre electronics, underneath boot, not damaged when running

Circuitry runs around base of boot

B.I.G. BOOST BOOTS

Suddenly, he heard voices in the hall outside. The Sharks had finished training and were coming back to their change room.

Zac was trapped!

CHAPTER ...FIVE

Thinking quickly, Zac squeezed himself inside an empty locker and pulled it shut. It was a very tight fit. He heard the Sharks come in to get changed and pack their bags.

'Hurry up!' snapped a voice.

I know that voice! That's Ms Sharpe, thought Zac. Ms Sharpe was Caz's mum.

She also worked for BIG.

'It's time to leave,' Ms Sharpe said. 'Make sure those balls are locked away before we go.'

Zac's spy senses tingled. Why would Ms Sharpe want the balls locked up? Tidied up, maybe – but locked up? *That sounds suspicious,* thought Zac.

Zac heard the players moving around, and gradually the change room fell silent. He stepped cautiously out of the locker.

Zac used his Wi-Fi wristband to dial Leon. He wanted to ask his brother about the soccer boots he'd found. Leon's face appeared on the tiny screen.

'Hi, Zac,' said Leon. 'What's up?'

'BIG are involved in this,' said Zac. 'Caz and Sharpe are here. I think they're using gadgets to cheat.'

'I wonder why?' said Leon. 'It seems like a lot of effort just for a trophy.'

'I know,' said Zac. 'It is weird, but I'll work it out. I've found some computer-controlled Boost Boots. Any ideas for deactivating them?'

'There's a gadget called an EMPump in your bag,' said Leon. 'It looks just like a ball pump, but it blows electro-magnetic pulses that freeze electronic devices.'

'Awesome,' said Zac. 'That should do it. See you, Leon!'

'Good luck,' said Leon.

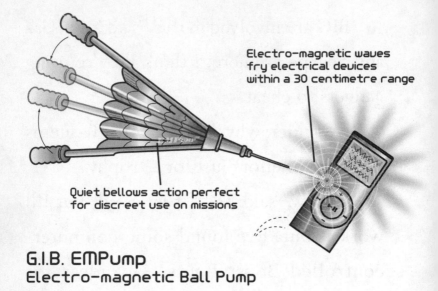

Electro-magnetic waves fry electrical devices within a 30 centimetre range

Quiet bellows action perfect for discreet use on missions

G.I.B. EMPump
Electro-magnetic Ball Pump

Zac hung up on Leon and unzipped his bag. He took out the EMPump and opened one of the lockers. Inside was a Sharks uniform and a pair of Boost Boots. Zac pointed the EMPump at the boots. He squeezed the pump's handles together. The pump beeped as it sent an invisible pulse through the air. Zac heard a faint buzz from the boots. He hoped that meant the EMPump had worked.

Zac opened every locker and shot an electro-magnetic pulse at each pair of boots. *They should be just like ordinary soccer boots now*, he thought.

Then Zac heard his coach yelling in the corridor. 'Where's Zav? he called. 'The team bus is leaving!'

Zac jumped up. He looked at the time.

He'd been way more than ten minutes! Zac swung his bag over his shoulder and ran for the door.

Just as he was leaving the change room, something on the floor caught his eye. It was a DVD. It looked like it had fallen out of a locker. Zac picked it up. It had the BIG logo on it! Underneath the logo, it said 'Recruitment ad – Top Secret'. Zac stuffed the DVD into his pocket as he ran out of the change room.

Coach was running down the player's ramp. 'There you are, Zav,' he said. 'Where in the world have you been? We've been looking everywhere.'

'Sorry – don't quite know my way

around yet,' said Zac, following Coach.

Coach led Zac to the bus outside. The rest of the players were already on board and chatting, excited after their training session. But Zac was distracted. He couldn't stop thinking about the DVD in his pocket.

The bus stopped out front of the High Towers Hotel. *Awesome!* thought Zac. He'd heard it was the fanciest hotel in Bladesville.

When the bus door opened, the Superstars' fans tried to climb onto the bus. Huge security guards dressed in orange jackets pulled them back.

This is nuts! thought Zac.

Zac followed his team mates out. Crowds of people waved and called out from all sides. The security guards held everyone back. Cameras flashed and girls screamed. Some fans were holding out autograph books for the players to sign.

Zac signed 'Zav Powski' over and over as he made his way up the stairs. No-one knew who he was, but they didn't seem to care. He was a Superstar!

Once they were all inside the hotel, the doors closed. The security guards blocked the entrance. 'No-one is getting in or out tonight,' said Coach. 'We are in lock-down. No reporters, no screaming fans.'

I guess that's all the spying I'll be doing today,

thought Zac. He had been hoping to slip out once everyone went to bed, but he could see there was no chance of that.

The team had dinner together. Zac was dying to get to his room so that he could check out the DVD.

Finally Zac told Coach he was tired from the training session and made his way to his room. He unlocked the door and walked in. He stopped dead, looking around. The room was huge! He had his own big screen TV and king-size bed.

Zac usually had to sleep in awkward and uncomfortable places on missions, if he got to sleep at all.

I could get used to being a professional soccer

player, thought Zac, grinning, as he took a running leap onto the bed.

CHAPTER... ...SIX

Zac took the DVD from his pocket and put it in the DVD player. Ms Sharpe appeared on the screen in her coaching outfit. She was smiling.

'Come on down to the Blackwood Improvement Ground to have some fun with your friends. Kick a ball around with your champions, the Sharks! Learn new skills in a safe, fun environment! And best of all, it's totally free!'

Zac was confused. BIG were starting a sports training centre? It didn't make sense. Then he remembered the label.

RECRUITMENT AD – TOP SECRET

Recruitment – of course! It wasn't a sports training centre – it was a BIG agent training centre! They'd be able to hand-pick agents from the kids that turned up to play sport.

Zac was sure he was right. But what did the grand final have to do with it?

Then it hit him. As well as the cash prize, the winning team would appear on

TV to get kids into sport. BIG would use this ad when the Sharks won. Everyone would think they were really generous, starting up a completely free training centre.

This was huge. Zac had to stop them. Even though he'd deactivated the Boost Boots, he knew BIG would have more tricks up their sleeve to win the grand final. They wouldn't leave anything to chance. Zac had to get a closer look at the Sharks' soccer balls before the match.

Zac lay back on the comfortable hotel bed. His muscles ached from the training session. He hadn't realised how tired he was. Zac closed his eyes. *I'll just have a little nap*, he thought.

Zac opened his eyes. He was in his hotel bed, and the morning sun was streaming through the window. It was grand final day! He sprang out of bed, determined to get to the stadium early.

Zac met the other Superstars downstairs for breakfast. There was a huge table covered with food. Zac piled his plate with toast, fruit and eggs. He poured himself a bowl of cereal as well. He was going to need all the energy he could get today.

After breakfast, the team took their bus back to the stadium. Everyone was talking about the big match. Zac wished he could get excited, but he had other things on his mind.

He glanced at his wristband.

He didn't have much time. He still needed to check out BIG's soccer balls.

The bus pulled up at the players' entrance to the stadium. Zac grabbed his bag. As soon as the door opened, he raced out of the bus.

'Hey, Zav!' called Coach. 'Where do you think you're going?'

'Toilet,' shouted Zac over his shoulder.

Zac ran across the playing field and down to the Sharks' change room again. His sharp eyes took everything in. In the corner, there was a giant Shark costume. It was the Sharks' mascot. It looked ridiculous.

He spotted something half-hidden behind a bench. Moving over, he saw that it was a soccer ball. The Sharks must have left it out accidentally when they locked up the others the night before.

He put down his bag and picked up the ball. It looked normal enough, except that it was covered in bulbous green patches. They looked like sensors of some kind.

A BIG logo was printed on it and there was a tiny control panel on its side.

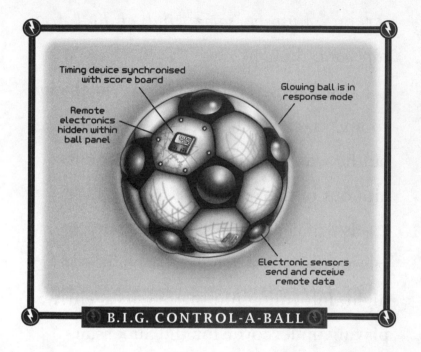

Timing device synchronised with score board

Remote electronics hidden within ball panel

Glowing ball is in response mode

Electronic sensors send and receive remote data

B.I.G. CONTROL-A-BALL

'What are you doing in my change room?' asked a mean-sounding voice behind Zac.

Zac spun around, dropping the ball.

Ms Sharpe was standing in the doorway! She was holding what looked like a touch screen. *Must be some kind of high-tech clipboard*, thought Zac.

'Just…um…I thought it was *our* change room,' said Zac. He knew it sounded lame, but he was counting on his disguise to get him out of there.

'Is that right?' she said, scowling. 'Don't take me for a fool! I received a phone call last night, informing me that a GIB agent was playing undercover for the Superstars.'

Uh-oh, thought Zac.

Ms Sharpe suddenly drew a line across her touch screen with a pen. The soccer ball on the floor flew at Zac.

Zac ducked quickly out of the way. Everything became clear to him in a second. Ms Sharpe could control the balls using her touch screen! *That's why those balls were changing direction during the Sharks' training yesterday!* thought Zac.

'Sorry,' said Zac, straightening up again and kicking the ball into the hallway, 'but you'll have to do better than that.'

Ms Sharpe smiled coldly and drew some more lines on her touch screen. A cupboard behind Zac sprang open. Four more balls bounced out towards him.

One after another, the soccer balls flew right at him. Zac kicked each one away before they could knock him down.

Despite his great jumps and scissor kicks, the balls kept coming back.

Ms Sharpe was drawing on her touch screen like crazy. One ball swerved in the air. Zac headed it away. But as the ball bounced off his forehead, something dropped on the floor. He lifted a hand to his face. His fake nose had been knocked off!

'Just as I thought,' said Ms Sharpe with a sneer. 'How nice to see you, Agent Rock Star.'

CHAPTER... ...SEVEN

Ms Sharpe started drawing all over her touch screen again. The balls flew towards Zac all at once. They spun around him in perfect circles. He felt like he was standing in a rotating tower.

I'm trapped in a cage made of flying soccer balls! thought Zac.

'Don't bother trying to kick the

Control-A-Balls away,' said Ms Sharpe, tucking her touch screen under her arm. 'They're set to formation.'

On her way out, Ms Sharpe picked up the Control-A-Ball that Zac had kicked into the hallway.

Zac tried kicking and hitting the spinning balls. But they just flew back to their original positions. He tried to squeeze between the balls but they whacked into him.

This is insane, he thought. *There has to be a way out of this.*

Zac could hear people starting to clap and cheer outside. He guessed the start of the game wasn't far away.

Zac put his hand in his pocket, searching for anything to get him out of the ball trap.

He pulled out a tiny bottle labelled 'Hydr8'. Zac quickly scanned the label.

Hydr8 is an H2O attracter.

A small amount of Hydr8 gel turns

into at least eight times its volume

of water. Simply squeeze into a

container and wait 30 seconds.

Ideal for use on desert missions.

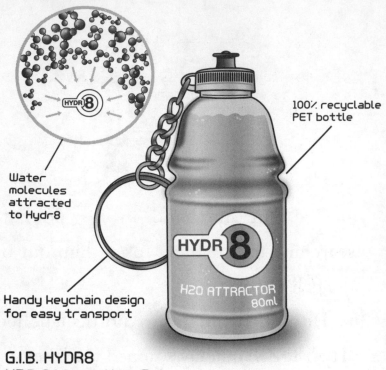

Water molecules attracted to Hydr8

100% recyclable PET bottle

Handy keychain design for easy transport

G.I.B. HYDR8 H2O Attracting Gel

Water! That gave Zac an idea. He knew that water and electricity didn't mix. He squeezed a tiny amount of the gel in the bottle into his hand. Cupping his other hand to form a bowl, he waited.

The seconds seemed like hours. Then all of a sudden he felt his hands getting wet. The gel was turning into water!

When Zac's hands were filled with water, he aimed as carefully as he could at one of the balls whizzing around him and threw the water over it.

ZZZZZKT!

The ball sparked and dropped to the floor. *Yes!* thought Zac.

He quickly squeezed some more gel onto his hands and did it again.

ZZZZZKT!

Another ball dropped down. Soon all four Contol-A-Balls were on the ground and Zac was free!

Zac heard the crowd cheering outside. The players' names were being announced through the stadium's loudspeakers. The game was about to start!

Zac ran over to where his fake nose was lying. The side that stuck to his skin was still sticky. He pushed it back onto his face and turned to run out of the room.

Ms Sharpe took a Control-A-Ball with her. That must be the ball they're playing with, thought Zac. *I've got to get her touch screen and destroy it. But now she knows who I am!*

Zac picked up the Sharks' mascot costume. He knew there were usually a few mascots dancing around the field. *Hmm… I might get close to Ms Sharpe in this.*

The costume had a blue body suit that went underneath a big foam shark suit. Zac put it on. His arms and legs stuck out of the shark's body, but his head was hidden inside the shark's head. There were eyeholes in the shark's mouth for him to see out.

Zac couldn't believe he might have to miss out on playing in the grand final, and instead complete his mission inside a shark suit. But the mission was way more important than a game of soccer.

Zac sighed as he caught sight of himself in a mirror. *The things I do for GIB!*

CHAPTER... EIGHT

Zac ran down the walkway and out onto the playing field. The stadium was packed. Thousands of people were looking down from the stands. He felt tiny standing beneath them. The sound of the crowd hummed in his ears.

Along one side of the field were benches for the teams and their coaches. There were a few other Sharks mascots dancing around near the Sharks' bench. Zac ran over towards them. Sharks' fans cheered at him from the stands.

Zac sighed to himself, and then began a funny dance. The crowd laughed as he jumped around, swinging his arms. Zac sneaked a quick look at the time on his wristband.

The referee in the middle of the soccer pitch blew his whistle.

The game was starting!

A Superstars player kicked off. The kick looked good to Zac, but it veered slightly off course. Instead of going to his team mate, the ball went straight to a Sharks player. The Sharks' fans went crazy, cheering and waving their flags.

Zac glanced at the Sharks' bench. Ms Sharpe was holding her pen and touch screen. He danced his way closer to her.

How am I going to get the touch screen off her? he wondered.

A Sharks player kicked the ball from halfway. Zac saw Ms Sharpe draw a curvy line with her pen. The soccer ball curved in the air in exactly the same way. It swerved

just out of the reach of the Superstars'
defenders and shot into the back of the
goal net.

The crowd went wild. The score was
$1 - 0$.

Zac did some more silly dancing to look
like he was happy. He skipped over to Ms
Sharpe. She had one arm raised, cheering
for the Sharks' goal. The touch screen was
under her other arm.

Zac had an idea. He grabbed Ms Sharpe's
arms and started to dance with her, like he
was celebrating the goal.

'What are you doing?' cried Ms Sharpe.
'Let go!'

But Zac held on tight and kept dancing,

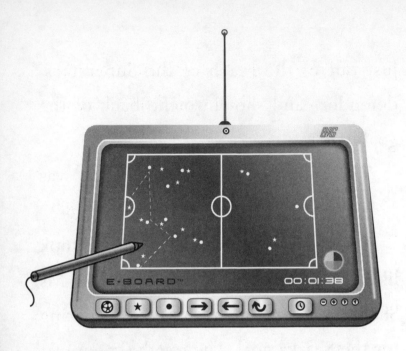

B.I.G. E-BOARD
Electronic Touch-screen Remote Control

more and more crazily. He spun Ms Sharpe in a circle. Her touch screen flew out from under her arm and crashed into the players' bench.

SMASH!

Ms Sharpe shook herself free from Zac

and ran over to pick it up. The screen had gone black. She shook it and tried drawing on the touch screen.

Zac looked at the ball on the field and crossed his fingers. Nothing happened. The ball was behaving like an ordinary soccer ball.

Ms Sharpe spun around and looked furiously at Zac.

'Get out of my sight!' she screamed.

Time to go, thought Zac with a grin. *My work here is done, anyway.*

Zac ran back to the change rooms and pulled off the shark costume. Then he ran back out onto the pitch and over to the Superstars' bench.

'Zav!' said Coach. 'Where have you been?'

'Sorry, Coach,' said Zac. 'I was... held up.'

'Never mind — get onto the field! We've got a game to win!' said Coach.

But just as Zac ran out onto the field, the referee blew his whistle for half-time. Without the Sharks' Boost Boots or Control-A-Ball, the score was locked at 1 − 0.

There was still time for the Superstars to win.

And I'm going to help them do it! thought Zac, determined.

CHAPTER NINE

Suddenly Zac's wristband beeped. A message appeared on its screen.

Good work Z. I am sitting in the front row. From L.

Zac looked for Leon in the crowd. He saw him wearing a nerdy tracksuit, sitting at the front. Leon was waving a Superstars flag. It was nice of him to come and watch.

Zac looked at his wristband.

We only need two goals to win, he thought.
The Superstars had a drink and a rest while
Coach talked to them about the first half
of the match.

PEEEEP!

Soon the referee blew his whistle and the
second half began. Without the Control-A-
Ball, the Sharks were playing terribly. One
player even missed the ball when he tried
to kick it.

Maybe they should have spent more time practising their skills and less time practising cheating, thought Zac, running hard across the field to get into position.

A Shark player kicked the ball out of bounds. A Superstar threw it back in over his head, landing it at Zac's feet.

Zac dribbled the ball through the midfield and around two Sharks defenders. He even kicked it between the legs of a player and kept control of it! Once in the clear, Zac kicked a cracking shot for goal.

The ball curved through the air as it flew towards Caz. She jumped for the ball with her arms outstretched. Caz looked set to miss, but the ball swerved into

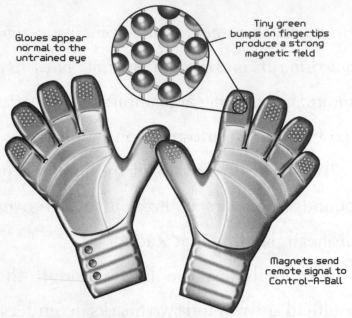

Gloves appear
normal to the
untrained eye

Tiny green
bumps on fingertips
produce a strong
magnetic field

Magnets send
remote signal to
Control-A-Ball

B.I.G. STICKY FINGERS
Magnetic Goalkeeping Gloves

her gloves at the last second.

She sneered at Zac, gripping the ball tightly. 'Better luck next time, Powski – or should I say Power?' Then she threw the ball to another Sharks player.

Zac looked at Caz's goalkeeping gloves.

He could just make out some tiny green bumps on the fingertips of the gloves. He suddenly remembered the strange green sensors he'd seen on the Control-A-Ball.

I bet they're programmed to attract the ball's sensors! he thought. *Just when I thought it was finally a fair match...*

As the game went on, the Superstars found it easy to outplay the Sharks. But Caz's gloves blocked all their shots on goal. The time was ticking away.

This is totally unfair, Zac thought. *I've got to find a way to score, or BIG will air their recruitment ad all over the country!*

A Superstar passed the ball to Zac. There was only one Shark defender to beat.

Zac ran around him and headed towards the goal. Caz was crouched and ready to use her magnetic gloves. Zac took the ball wide to one side of the goal. Caz followed, blocking his way.

'Zav!'

Out of the corner of his eye, Zac saw one of his team mates, standing on the other side of the goal.

Zac passed him the ball. Caz had left too much of the goal unguarded. She jumped too late. Zac's team mate pounded the ball past her. It smacked into the back of the net. 1 – 1. The scores were level!

Fans jumped up and down in the stands. The Superstars gave each other high fives.

I guess Caz needs to be close to the ball for her magnetic gloves to work, thought Zac.

The referee restarted the game from the centre. There was only a minute or so left on the clock. Zac took control, racing the ball down the left wing. He dodged Sharks players as he went.

'Zav! Zav! Zav!' chanted the crowd.

Suddenly, a Sharks player tripped Zac. Zac went flying to the ground.

'Better luck next time,' said the Shark.

The referee blew his whistle and held up a yellow card.

'Zav!' called a Superstar, 'you were fouled inside the penalty box! You have a free shot at goal!'

Sharks players ran over to the referee to complain. The Superstars' fans were cheering.

Zac stood up and carried the ball to the penalty spot. Caz stared straight at him.

'No-one can help you this time,' she said. 'I can block any shot you make.'

Zac ignored her. He had to focus.

The crowd stood on their feet as Zac took a deep breath. He ran up to the ball and kicked it with all his might.

CHAPTER... ...TEN

SMACK!

The ball shot towards Caz like a comet. She caught it in front of her chest. For a split second Caz smiled. But Zac had kicked the ball so hard, it pushed her backwards! She landed at the back of the goal net, still holding the ball. She looked dazed and confused.

The crowd went wild. Zac pulled his shirt over his head and ran around the pitch like a maniac.

'WOO-HOO!'

He had never felt so excited. The Superstars ran up to Zac and leapt on top of him.

The siren for the end of the game sounded across the stadium. It was all over. The Superstars had won, 2 – 1!

'I caught it! I caught it!' yelled Caz above the noise.

'It was a nice catch,' called Zac, 'but the ball still crossed the goal line.'

Zac looked at Ms Sharpe. She was sitting on the Sharks' bench, looking furious.

The crowd was going crazy, cheering and singing and laughing. The Superstars went over to shake hands with the Sharks. Zac heard a beep from his Wi-Fi wristband. It was a message from Leon.

Nice goal, Zac!

Zac grinned and waved to Leon in the crowd. TV cameras circled the players, filming Zac and his team mates celebrating.

Then the announcer spoke over the stadium's sound system. 'We will now present the trophy to the winning team.'

The players gathered below a stage that had been set up in the middle of the soccer pitch. Zac looked around but couldn't see

Caz or Sharpe. They had slipped away in the excitement.

Oh well, he thought. *At least I managed to stop BIG from recruiting more kids into their evil agency.*

The announcer walked up to the microphone on the stage. He was holding a golden trophy.

The crowd hushed.

'Congratulations to the Superstars,' he said. 'I am pleased to present this trophy to the player of the match, Zav Powski!'

Everyone cheered even louder than before. Zac climbed the stairs to the stage and shook the announcer's hand. He held up the trophy. His team mates jumped around him. Yellow and blue streamers flew through the sky. Photographers lined up to snap photos of the winning team. Zac smiled as cameras flashed in his direction.

'Thank you,' said Zac into the microphone. 'It was a great game. The Superstars play hard and they play fair.'

The crowd cheered again.

After the ceremony, Coach came over to talk to Zac. 'You're still young but you're an excellent player,' he said. 'How would you like to join the Superstars for good?'

Zac was stunned. Become a professional sports star? Zac opened his mouth to answer. But then he closed it again.

Hang on, he thought, *I already have the best job in the world.*

'Thanks, Coach,' said Zac. 'But I think I'll retire early.'

Coach looked surprised. Zac handed him the trophy and walked away. He found Leon examining the Control-A-Ball.

'Quite clever, actually,' Leon said. 'The way the short-range sensors were attracted to the electrogmagnets in –'

'We should probably get going, Leon,' interrupted Zac, rolling his eyes. His brother was such a geek!

They sneaked away from the crowds and went down to the change room. Leon gave Zac a bag of clothes. Zac got changed and pulled off his silicone nose. He messed up his hair how he liked it.

'That's better!' said Zac.

They walked back up to the field. The crowds were beginning to thin out. Mr Kane walked past them. Zac groaned under his breath. He had just remembered the training session that Mr Kane had signed him up for.

'Zac!' he said, ticking Zac's name off his clipboard. 'I'm glad you're here. Wasn't it a great game?'

'It sure was, sir,' said Zac, trying not to look too pleased with himself.

'The Superstars are running the special

training session now,' said Mr Kane, pulling him in the direction of his classmates. 'Come on – you'll be able to learn a lot from that Zav Powski player. What a star!'

... **THE END** ...

For freebies, downloads
and info about other
Zac Power books, go to

www.zacpower.com

MISSION CHECKLIST
How many have you read?